I0664384

Shorts: A Moratorium On The Ordinary

Shorts: A Moratorium On The Ordinary

Short stories to entertain the busy, yet
complicated mind.

Dedicated to Mr. Jim Campbell, my high school metal shop teacher. He understood my creativity, need for freedom, and the confusion inherent in a young mind.

Shorts: A Moratorium On The Ordinary

Shorts: A Moratorium On The Ordinary

Written, illustrated, and published by Steven Reed Dahlquist

Sketch Master app used for photo effects

Contact: stevenreeddahlquist@gmail.com

ISBN-13: 978-0-9977918-2-2

Content Ratings
AA—All audiences
NC—Not for children
MR—Mature readers/graphic content

The Blade (MR)...12

Paperclips (MR)..25

Wrecked (MR)...30

Six Thirty Coffee (MR) 33

The Mechanism (NC)....................................37

The Mask (AA)..41

The Message (NC)...58

Stillness And Terror (NC) 63

Under My Bed (AA)......................................65

Voices (NC) 68

The Resume (NC)..70

Pretty Box (NC)...73

One Step Forward And Two Steps

Back (NC)...78

Upside Down Smile (AA)............................83

The Misunderstood Spoon (AA)................87

Geoff The French Lover (MR)....................94

New Man (NC)...98

The Woman With Six And A

Half Foot Feet (AA).....................................108

A Day In The Life (AA)...............................123

Countdown (NC)...128

Neat And Tidy (NC).....................................131

Floyd: A Case Study (NC)...........................139

Aurelia's Story (AA).....................................145

The Unwelcome Visitor (NC)....................147

Never Born (NC)..151

Crash (AA) 156

Sand God (AA)..157

Woman In The West Of Iceland (NC).......158

Thorn In My Heart (NC)..............................160

The Ancient Friend (AA)............................161

Random Guy (NC).......................................162

The Search (NC)..163

Shorts: A Moratorium On The Ordinary

The Stories begin now.

The Blade

Coop beheld The Blade when he first walked in through the guitar shop's squeaky-hinge door. Placed there on the burnt-orange carpeting, it was surrounded by other instruments, seemingly positioned to give homage to this femme fatale. As if it possessed some eerie sense of self-awareness and uncanny ability to command its surroundings, it fulfilled its all-consuming lust for life. Perhaps it was destiny; at that moment Coop knew wild horses could not keep him from it.

There was no price tag; it didn't matter. The Blade was his, save the transaction. Price was no object. Besides, it looked well used. The underlying wood grain showed in sizable highlights around the edges where the glossy-black paint had worn through, so it couldn't cost much.

One feature that caught his attention was the reddish, flat-wooden projection with a pointed tip extending upward from the tuner head. The guitar had character. Coop thought it odd, nevertheless, his name was written all over it.

Awed, he reverently picked it up, savoring the swill as he sipped of its sweet intrigue. Though distracted by what lay in his hands, he found his way to the old, wood paneling-covered sales counter, and said, "How much?"

From behind the counter, a gaunt, man with waterfall-like streamers of gray interspersed in his long dark hair, deep-set eyes, and a black Henley T-shirt, peered at him below the brim of a red baseball cap. Sustaining his gaze for a time well beyond what is comfortable for most people, Coop felt uneasy.

In a deep-raspy voice the man said, "There is no price...now. She can neither be bought nor sold. She's not owned, but owns. She decides who, and when. Take her and go. Or, do yourself a favor, junior, and don't."

*   *   *

Nobody knows why she's called The Blade,

but I do. If I didn't, I wouldn't be telling you this story, because really, it's none of your goddamn business. Nevertheless, your curiosity's piqued, so here's her story.

Anastasia was a luthier—of electric guitars—well known in her trade by the late 1960's, and by any measure, an artist as well as an accomplished player. Her husband, Pierre, was a man's man, who cared for her above all and everything else. He had Anastasia's name and image tattooed over much of his upper body; and that was back in the day when stick-and-poke was a common way of blazing one's manliness.

No man would lay a hand on Anastasia. All knew better, since one had tried but didn't live to tell about it—a story for another day. She was a fair woman. So fair, that many entertained the idea in their minds, but wisely left it there.

A man of dark renown had come to town. He was a big, olive-skinned man, with a plethora of facial scars. Nothing was sacred to him, including Anastasia. Pierre was no more than something to move aside. Which, one night, he did.

As the man busted through their bedroom door, squeezing off rounds from his Colt 45, Pierre was caught off guard. The moments of chaos left him mortally wounded.

When the dust settled, he lay on the floor, bloody, at the end of his life. One could not say if the wetness around his eyes and face was sweat, or tears for not having been able to protect his wife by fending off this bastard. There's no doubt in my mind it was the latter. He died a miserable, helpless death.

The stranger had his way with her. He spent a few hours in that house, during which he raped Anastasia repeatedly. There wasn't much left of her when he finally finished getting what he wanted. The brazen son of a bitch left the door open as he casually walked out.

Despite the torment and sustained injuries, she came-to after a couple of hours, partly because of the cold of the night. Her insides were aflame. Both eyes were blackened from the accompanying beating for her resistance, and a part of her lower lip was bitten off, still bleeding. Within this abattoir-like scene, one couldn't exactly say where all she was injured. The drying blood shone from the streetlights through the window—the blinds having been left asunder in the struggle.

Purpose-filled, she managed to stumble the way into her shop. Taking from the shelf the black guitar she had made for Pierre—it was a flawless work of art, crafted especially for him—she determined that it would be her weapon of revenge. Onto the body of the guitar she painted, "The Blade," with her quivering hands.

They say that criminals return to the scene of the crime. She was counting on it. Had he not, she would have gone looking for him, or died trying. The heavy footsteps on their wooden porch alerted her of his return. This time she was the one who had the element of surprise.

Standing in the dark room until after he entered, she exploded a roundhouse across his head with The Blade. He fell to the floor as she swung the instrument around for another head blow. Knocking him half silly, she whirled it around again and sunk the edge deeply into his back. The following rage-filled strike was across his upper arm, breaking it clean through causing him to roll over from the shock and awe.

The next target of her erupting furor was his knee; the kneecap was left broken and mostly detached, hanging out of the skin by a single ligament from the fibula.

Lying there bloody and beaten, he pleaded for his life. She answered decisively with seven more enraged blows to the crown of his head. Brains on the floor, and spattered on the walls and herself, she turned around and mournfully, as well as painfully, carried Pierre's guitar back to her shop.

After sitting for a few moments, she fashioned a pointed blade from a piece of maple. Then she solidly fixed it to the head of The Blade. Placing the pointed tip just below her sternum, she whispered to her lover, "Forgive me Pierre," and fell prone on it.

As consciousness faded, her thoughts of Pierre accompanied her as she was also ushered to oblivion.

There are always evil men, who seem to work at making life hell for others. I don't believe they think about it, but are, for whatever reason, uncaring sons-a-bitches. That bastard deserved to die, and most likely many times over. May his afterlife, if there is one, be one of equal recompense, if that were possible.

*   *   *

Coop got home, plugged in and strummed her. She was as smooth as a southern breeze. He had never played a guitar that had such a stratty sound. No, "stratty" didn't do it justice, he thought; it had its own sound.

*   *   *

Sounds, much like colors, are difficult qualities to describe, without using comparisons. Go ahead and try to describe purple, or the moo of a cow. Don't spend much time on it, it can't be done. The Blade sounded like The Blade. Its sound was its own.

More importantly, when heard, it filled the chosen hearer with a penumbra of fervor that was felt, but not understood. It tugged at their heartstrings: a mélange of feelings--of melancholy and of rage.

*   *   *

Playing non-stop, the blood from his fingers mingled with the strings and fretboard, yet he stayed. Late that night, exhaustion demanded he and his sanguine fingers rest.

Sleep didn't come easily to him, his mind filled with morose thoughts.

*   *   *

The coroner determined that Pierre and Anastasia had no known family members, so their estate was transferred to the courts for liquidation at auction to the highest bidder. I attended that auction. It was there that I got The Blade. Some residual blood lay in the joints and chinks, but someone had the decency to wipe it down after it was used to brain the nameless murderer.

That auction is where I first strummed it, and the first-and-last time it would be bought or sold. It had to be sold once, seemingly to represent the value of the murderer's life.

When the auctioneer got to The Blade, no one bid. The dark story and residual blood was a bit much for the constitution of most. The auctioneer's starting bid went down, and down.

Seeing there was no interest, he offered it at one cent. I thought I had just gotten a ridiculously good deal, but soon afterward I found out the real cost.

I got home, plugged in, and strummed her again. She was as smooth as a southern breeze. I had never played such a guitar. It had its own sound.

Playing incessantly for hours, the blood from my fingers mingled with the strings, fretboard, and the residual blood from the lamentable event, yet I stayed. Late that night, exhaustion demanded that I rest myself and my bloody fingers. Sleep didn't come easily; my mind was filled with morose thoughts.

*   *   *

Coop got enough rest that his body was willing to respond. He bandaged his fingers, then played for hours, through the evening, and into the night. Something drove him to stay, even well-nigh late. Perhaps it was the sound, or maybe the emotions that accompanied it. It was both, it was all, it was the quintessence of Anastasia's mortal existence, and the ethereal manifestation of her posthumous state. It was compelling, undeniable, and could in no way be disavowed.

Day after day, the young guitarist maintained the rigor, never stopping to eat, and took only minimal sleep. After 17 days, his body collapsed and his mind went into a state of tilt-overload.

Coop slept straight through four days, after which time he felt a release from the instrument's spell. He spent a couple of days regaining his strength before he did what he knew he had to do.

*   *   *

Day after day I played The Blade; not stopping for food, taking only enough sleep to satisfy my body's undeniable needs. I had kept up this ritual for 22 days before I collapsed with consummate fatigue.

Five days I slept. When I woke, there was a release of some kind, where I knew I was finished with The Blade; my time had come, and gone. That was years ago. I set it there in my shop where Coop, and untold others have seen it. From the look in his eyes, I knew he was the next one through which it, she, whatever, would live.

I can't explain it. But I've seen it enough times, and experienced it myself—there's a spiritual connection with just a few people. No, not everyone looks at The Blade and is moved as with Coop, and myself. Most people see it, look puzzled, and go back to whatever they were doing.

But know this, She's not a killer. She wants to live, but not at the expense of another. She'll use you until you can take no more, then release you. She'll find another. She always finds another.

*   *   *

Coop languidly walked back to the guitar shop and through the squeaky-hinge door. This time he wasn't there to look. He was there to deliver The Blade back to the awaiting stand, there in the middle of the shop, on the burnt-orange carpet, surrounded by other guitars, seemingly giving it homage.

He looked up at the shop owner behind the wood paneling-covered sales counter. They sustained their gaze for a time, well beyond what feels comfortable to most people, but now he understood. Coop looked away and, without a word, walked out, annunciated by the squeaky-hinge door.

Paperclips

No one suspected. It had been 13 years of clandestine daily collecting. Albeit, none would have cared. Each night's work culminated with the completion of his acquisition operation, as subtle, unobtrusive, and even silly as it was. One from this desk today, one from that one next week—rotating through each workstation so as to raise no suspicion.

The 23 years he had been with the company felt like twice that, the last 13 of which saw him filled with bitterness. Nevertheless, he'd accumulated more than enough to accomplish his mad-as-a-March-hare plan.

Clive was a simple man, though many who didn't know better thought him to be a simpleton—one could perhaps make a reasonable argument leading to that conclusion, but we'll leave that to those who enjoy a good-unsolicited judgement. He was reliable, and by all accounts, the worker bees enjoyed the fruits of his character.

Within his soul there resided an empty space, formerly filled by his wife until she moved on to fill another man's similar empty space. A man with whom she left at the end of the company party—one that Clive resented having attended. She never returned.

Besides, it seemed more like an exercise in humility, or at least an outward expression of such, to have invited him at all. The culmination of the evening with her departure, broke his heart in such a profound way that it would never be set right.

That was the time when the resentment began, during which he first developed his morbid scheme. That was also the time when he began to purposefully gather the paper clips, one at a time.

Working the typical janitorial night shift, there was never an opportunity for morale-building chit chat around the water dispenser. For many who worked there, Clive was a mostly-unseen entity that magically kept the bathrooms, and the blue office carpeting

clean. There wasn't anybody to say hello to, or mutually avoid eye contact. Just "the cleaning guy," as he was sometimes referred, and not necessarily with affection, as judgement tends to creep in against the lesser of professions.

On the rare occasion that he was briefly spotted after a long pull to finish the nightly routine, there wasn't much evidence of any relationship. Even so, the heavy spirit that had become Clive's, was evident to all who possessed even the least powers of perception. No one paid much attention to it, but simply assumed that during his life he had been through a "lot." That may have been true, but the man who took his wife likely had more to do with it than the speculated "lot."

Fiddling one morning years ago, he discovered that if he straightened a paper clip, bent it into a U-shape, then triple-twisted the two ends together, he could link them into a relatively strong chain. Liberally estimating, he determined that it would take about twelve to comprise a length of one foot.

He established a goal of one foot of chain for each year of service, which, much like the way he felt about his job, was more than enough. Some quick multiplication determined that he would need 276 jumbo-size paper clips to pull this off.

Though Clive was not a big man, his weight was adequate so that the small-gauge wire excoriated the skin of his neck sufficiently to cause a bloody shambles.

One certainly could not argue that the posthumous mess that remained equaled the sum total of cleaning he had performed over his 23 years, but could in fact establish the case that he generated a right-good one, both physically and in the minds of those early arrivers who found him.

Wrecked

He wrecked her. While she'd spent her life with a reasonable amount of confidence, he wrecked her. He was bad news from the beginning, but she seemed to gravitate toward his type.

Fully disdaining herself and her existence, and having wholly lost every tittle of self respect, she didn't go out. Even in her present mental condition she knew enough to not want others to see her bruises, as she knew it would be tantamount to a silent cry for help. Even though the self-inflicted burns and needle marks could be hidden, shame checkmated.

She remained in her dingy room—god forbid he should come home unexpectedly and find her gone; there'd be hell to pay. It would be the usual: he'd beat her, then rape her, though she would have to feign pleasure to avoid escalation. It was all so reprehensible, yet familiar.

The needle marks were by her choice. They seemed a better, more effective mate than alcohol, which to a smaller degree was also part of her mind-consoling regimen. There was no apparent escape, at least not at the risk of enduring more beatings.

Though she didn't want to die, she upped a drop, wanting only to press the envelope of life to see if there might be an escape—she was afraid; she was desperate. That's when he came home.

She didn't expect his odious ass until later, but the door flew open and he stood there with the same look of disdain that she had for herself. Her heavy dose was kicking in, and that's when the beating began. Their separate dysfunctions converged for another page of their hideous alliance.

Somehow her heightened trip paralleled his heightened rage. The beating seemed for an eternity, as she moaned, half unconscious and half consciously enduring the hate-conveying blows.

He loosened his belt and dropped his pants; she harkened back to childhood; her father came into her the same way. Hatred for her father, herself, and this beast on top of her filled her erupting sensibilities.

Having both an awareness of the infliction, and herself fading away to oblivion, time quickened. He climaxed, and her consciousness went gray as he withdrew his penis. Darkness followed the gray, and the end of her life followed the darkness. It was a shitty day.

Six-Thirty Coffee

The two met every morning for coffee at 6:30. He and she had maintained the routine for years. Both expected the other would take the reins of the relationship and trot their way to destiny—she more than he. Nevertheless, the years passed and coffee remained the anchor of their connection. There was nothing else.

There was no relational battlefield, and no predictable expectation beyond the benign coffee experience—tepid black liquid dripping down their respective throats, as if it were an oral IV.

Though never spoken, both knew they had reached the epitome of their relationship. Yet they talked of what was to come, wished for what could be, and habitually repeated the ritual with exacting regularity.

All the while, he pondered what it would be like to suck on her nipples—specifically if he could get both of them in his mouth at once—and she thought about his face nestled into her breasts, with both nipples in his mouth sucking them like a sledgehammer.

Smiling to herself as he talked, she considered her mixed metaphor, realizing that metaphors don't have to be spoken, but can be merely thought. This initiated a twinge of a smile, to which she drew no attention, and he thought it was something he had said.

Neither would be so audacious as to suggest having sex, or migrate their relations in such an a-religious direction, which echoed negatively in their minds from early life training.

Sipping her coffee and carrying on conversation, she imagined going out with him for a drink. Returning to his place, he would throw her on his bed, unbuckle the belt on his faded ripped-denim jeans, and penetrate her with forceful undulations. He imagined the same.

They shared the same thoughts, though unknown to one another—each living in their own mind, having an identical parallel experience but never together. It was a sad irony.

It was Friday, 6:54 am. Having independently become mutually dissatisfied with the benign relationship which was theirs, each had decided to break it off for a while. He began to speak first, but yielded when she began to speak, because he could think of no reason to jump into the fire of what he wanted to tell her.

She paused, realizing he had spoken first, but then continued at his prompt for her to go ahead. "I feel like we might take a break from meeting for a while," slightly lifting her right cheek and brow, and tilting her head as she finished, giving it the feel of a question more than a statement; she was feeling insecure about herself and her motivations, and really just wanted to have sex with him.

His beige corduroy sportcoat-clad arms loosely crossed on the bistro table, and feet flat on the floor, he nodded slightly as he looked into her eyes. "Okay, sure, I understand. Maybe that's best," he replied;

and though he was not feeling insecure about himself, he knew what he really wanted was to have sex with her.

That night they sat alone in their respective apartments and watched television; the next day, neither of them could remember what they watched. Each made their own coffee, had only a sip or two, then poured the rest down the drain.

The Mechanism

Fiercely independent, Eiger took both pleasure and pride in doing things for himself. He seemed to have an innate confidence in his hands to complete whatever his mind conceived. What he needed for his various and sundry projects would almost magically present itself--if not specifically, then something that would do the job, with an added creative tweak. This skill, along with his willingness to help others, made him locally famous as an all-around good man to know.

He marched to the beat of a drum that others couldn't hear. His banner was creativity, and its stanchion, his independent nature. Most people being the followers that they are, and typically unable to perceive the creative's rhythmic percussions, viewed him as likable but unusual. Nevertheless, he was always in good spirits, inspiring those in his community so that they were pleased when they saw him.

Eiger didn't feel unusual, but he could rationally observe his different way of thinking. He was never found being trendy, or following the crowds. He alone decided what he would do and when he would do it. Once he decided, based on how he felt about it and how it rested in his balances of justice, there was no redirecting him.

Paradoxically, he knew that his mind would wander, and following a wandering leader would result in, well, wandering. That wandering manifested as bouncing from this thought to that thought in a moment, leaving him surrounded by a plethora of incomplete thoughts, unfinished projects, and an incessant state of mental disorganization.

During his service in the armed forces earlier in his life, he obtained his chaplaincy, which translated to officiating the joining of many in holy matrimony, the final laying to rest of others, and offering therapy to those in between.

For these occasional services he never charged, but rather considered it a gift and therefore his duty to mankind. Naturally, this endeared him to the community, however sometimes, he did feel taken for granted, but not so much that he withdrew; he would always say yes, and do so with a smile.

Growing older and not so many years from the day of his final sunset, he began to make plans for his own funeral. Being a man who was quick to help others, but reticent to ask, he began to form a plan to take care of his own funeral without the need to bother others—the ones to whom he had so freely given, not thinking how laughable that was. Nevertheless, plan he did, working out the technical and mechanical details, right down to the tombstone.

It was an incredible feat of shade-tree engineering. With the simple pull of a cord, conveniently located at a depth of five feet, the displaced soil positioned strategically on a hinged mechanism using gravity, rather like a dump truck, would return the earth to the intended grave.

Soil replaced, the spring-loaded tombstone was allowed to rise and permanently lock into place, which in turn released the rake to apply the finishing touch across the grave, as if performed under the supervision of an undertaker.

Lying at the bottom of the gravesite, holding the terminal handle of the pull cord, as if to feel the sensation he might experience just at the moment of his death when his arm would drop, thereby setting into motion the mechanical sequence, Eiger became captivated by singing birds.

The walls of the grave seemed to amplify and enhance their collective songs. He didn't expect such resonating sounds of nature to surround him in what would eventually be his final moments.

Listening and considering the perfection of it all, in an instant he became drowsy. His eyelids became infinitely heavy, and he momentarily nodded off. His arm dropped, the jerk of which startled him awake just as the burial sequence engaged.

Birds were singing, the sky blue, and all with mild temperatures. Unattended, as planned, it was a beautiful day for a funeral.

The Mask

Though compelled by cultural stereotypes to search for food during the cover of darkness, the bandits preferred to search in the daylight. Time and tradition had solidly established them to be filchers of whatever they found, picked, or caught. For this reason his kind were thought to be nocturnal—it was the mask.

Small compared to his peers, at just nine months Gary was already showing himself to be a precocious bandit. He'd steal a fish or bottle cap here, pinch a slug or hair clip there, lift a dropped bit of cupcake or potato chip at the park, or rob a wild blackberry or garden carrot in season. He stole more than he could use.

Honest gain had no meaning to the raccoon clan—Gary and his kind all knew themselves to be thieves; it had been millennia since any of them might have thought otherwise. Furthermore, the quality of what they stole had no meaning to them. It didn't matter if it was made in Paris, or Paducah, as long as it was edible or shiny. Likewise, how they went about getting things had no meaning, no matter the destruction or harm inflicted.

At a glance, raccoons as a species appear docile, even cute. But don't cross them, or their vicious alter ego will emerge, baring sharp, rabies-ridden teeth that can flay an area of a leg or other body part in a few short seconds, oftentimes initiating a slow, hydrophobic death. This was the profound threat their society could lord over others— an abundantly real peril in the minds of all, save the most ferocious or those with the densest fur.

Some animals were interested in his shiny things, but nearly all were interested in his food, and willing to pay well. For some it was because they wanted to please, in hopes of being socially accepted—one of the in-crowd. Most of those who weren't interested, by virtue of their natural food preferences or their emotional resistance to control, could be persuaded otherwise.

Members of feral societies, or arguably all societies, incline toward fitting in; the desire for social approval via conformance, partaking of a belief system (spiritual or otherwise), loyalty to the bourgeoisie, virtue flagging, and socially-popular memberships are all indicative of this.

Even so, what massaged Gary's ego the most in this *ménage de la nature*, was the feeling of control he was gaining over the other members of society. The potential had found its potentate, opening the door to a new natural order, which to most didn't feel so natural. His kudzu of domination was about to propagate to the far corners of his autocratic arboretum, in soils richly amended by fear.

*   *   *

Soon engaging a coterie of minions, Gary found popularity and power, and not, mind you, because he was Adonis reborn. The small-sharp teeth, the beady, narrow-set eyes, the pointy nose that looked like it wanted to be stuck into everyone else's business, and the narrow shoulders set against the oversized haunches did not differentiate him as a charismatic leader.

Nevertheless, it was well-suited to his psyche, as witnessed by his sadistic notoriety.

Benny was the first initiate of the new-found order, and was a certifiable live wire. Whatever Gary told him to do, he did, and if it meant dishing out the Gary-flavor of justice, he was all in.

Another of his opportunistic followers was called Gizzard. His epithet was of dark origins, but also one that endeared him to Gary. He had a peculiar sadistic bent for extracting a bird's gizzard in a rather surgical way, and then flinging it—his version of *catch and release*. After which he stayed apprised of its whereabouts as it scratched its way toward death. In the final moments, he ate the tortured victim alive. It was gruesome, but Gary's demented posse found it amusing.

Not all of his cohort were so malevolent. Chigger was one such member. Not caring for the leverage that came with the job, he only wanted to be accepted and liked. Many were like Chigger, doing any pleasing thing to get the approval of Gary.

As the leader of this new movement, the direction of which he dictated, his main interest was in number one. He was clever, even brilliant, but lacked the balance of altruism, or even kindness, to make having those qualities socially favorable: a classic case of greatest strength and greatest weakness; any unmitigated strong quality is unbalanced, thereby essentially being a rationale for evil.

That was Gary's downfall, and what allowed his conscience to take a pass on mercy, leaving their feral society in a state of tension. Divergent from the former freedom and peace they had always known, it was gone with the setting sun. Change would be on the morning horizon.

*   *   *

No more nocturnal feeding for the 'coon clan, at least not on Gary's watch. Becoming as thick as thieves, their banner was pride; where pride didn't guide, threats did. They weren't empty or hopeful threats; Gary demanded loyalty, and the price of acting out otherwise was certain death. Crossing him was not allowed, and he never erred on the side of understanding or kindness, because he had neither. When he did make an "example" of someone, their carcass was left on display to be picked at by vultures and decomposed by worms so as to dilate the impact.

Gary had a number of sows with whom he would satisfy his drive, all of which were expected to be monogamous. The spawn grew to be wild like their father.

In fact, Gary was almost always off with his syndicate, strengthening their position and collecting pizzo, or protection money, which by Gary's declaration was pine nuts or wild blueberries—the former being a favorite food staple, as well as the latter, but the blueberries had an additional quality; they could be fermented into a sporting beverage.

For some members of society, like squirrels, gathering pine nuts was a snap. Woodpeckers and crossbills could collect their nuts with a little more effort. But for the others it was mostly impossible, yet they still had to pay. This was the beginning of black market nuts.

Squirrels exchanged nuts for green pine cones. This allowed them to concentrate on their work in safety—many lost their lives having slipped and fallen from the upper branches. They only knew to work and work quickly. Not that bright, they were content with being allowed to keep half of their bounty.

Their special protection included being spared further pizzo. They would simply be protected. The squirrels never asked what they were being protected from, but silently went to work, giving an occasional bark to announce predators—the insurance program didn't cover predators.

Most members of society could collect blueberries, accommodating those unable to disassemble cones. This currency developed into a complex system of specialization.

The birds could collect blueberries, or knock down the cones to sell to the moles in exchange for worms. The moles in turn sold them to the squirrels for nuts. The foxes promised the squirrels protection from predators and established a shift schedule to fulfill that promise. Unfortunately, the sly nature of the foxes would occasionally surface, showing their true colors—eating those they were guarding.

Being generally non-social, the squirrels were indifferent about those whose demise eventuated between the teeth of a fox.

The hawks and owls would trade voles to the foxes for nuts that they got from the squirrels.

Some would add value to their currency by making pine nut pesto, sun-roasting the nuts, or fermenting blueberries into wine.

Incidentally, the bears repugnantly shook their heads and ignored what they thought of as silly drama. For the most part, outside of the bears, everyone found a niche that could be filled in order to appease Gary. Still, there was no peace, or contentment.

Benny, Gizzard, and a new 'coon member, Cisco, did most of the collections and enforcement. The worst part is that they enjoyed it. The cries for mercy from clients meant nothing. The results were odious; the three joked about how the bugs and worms gotta eat too, laughing as they went about their way.

Sometimes cruelty can magnify under group influence. We all have a dark side and endeavor to keep it under wraps, but when a mob mentality rules, it can be unleashed and given freedom to go wild.

*   *   *

Money typically has no intrinsic value. It's worth lies in the willingness of those who use it, to value and exchange. Neither does money make one rich, but rather it's a measure of wealth.

Wealth is no more than access to desired goods, from the best hollowed out tree or fallen log, to the amount and quality of food. Society determines the acceptability of currency.

Gary had more pine nuts than he could fill himself with for years. He ate an enormous amount, but to him and society, his great accumulation represented importance, power, and the control of virtually everything. It fed his oversized ego in his undersized body.

What made it work for him was the synergy of intelligence, cleverness, desire for control, and abject lack of empathy—a combination unique to him. He took what he wanted then demanded more in his unquenchable thirst for wealth and power.

Realizing he had pushed his fees and controls to the limits of what society could sustain, he began to look for other ways to up his take. That's when the issuing of permits began.

The others were made to feel like they were getting something for their money, since they knew that the protection concept was a sham, nothing more than a way for Gary to forcibly take what was theirs.

Now, a permit was required for everything. Worms needed a permit for micro-excavation. The squirrels needed a "Severance of Integration" permit, which came to be called the "Dis," short for disintegration, before stripping pine cones.

The bears were given a complimentary "Right to Passage" permit, which delineated their Gary-given permission to do whatever, whenever. Furthermore, they were never required to display or carry their permit. It was Gary's way of sending a message to society that he had determined it best for everyone if the bears followed the strictly uninhibited freedom allowed by said permit (which could be found littered around the forest).

Once permits were assigned to all, in accordance with the new statutes, a new tax was instituted.

The Peace Tax had one purpose: to deepen Gary's already deep pockets. It was concealed under the guise of promoting social order, to which most gave credence. But not the bears—they saw right through the attempt to obscure the true motives, and could not understand why the others could not.

The Peace Tax, as presented and enforced, required that all would get along peacefully. Any disturbance of the peace would result in a tax, albeit small, "to all parties involved or determined to be involved by virtue of proximity to said disturbance," to be exacted by duly appointed members of the Peace Enforcement Team (PET).

Some disturbances were the result of over-consuming fermented blueberry drink. Drinking translated into increased revenue, ergo, it was not discouraged, neither encouraged—minimizing accusations of hypocrisy.

Hypocrisy is a quality best avoided when in a leadership position. Leaders displaying such behavior tend to move the masses toward rebellion. When placed onto the societal balances, equity with such leaders comes up wanting when measured against expectations. This behavior is not overlooked for long, but becomes a nagging goad, giving rise to unrest.

Gary understood and avoided it, not wanting to provoke those he tenuously controlled. Not that he was worried about an imminent rebellion, but in leadership there is always that risk when the masses are pressed toward aggravation, no matter how gently. In such a state of affairs, the leader is the one who ultimately loses.

With the simultaneous institution of both the property tax on living quarters, and the personal property tax on possessions, murmurs of displeasure began. Members of society felt burdened with indiscriminate taxation, and that without representation.

*   *   *

Gary called all the shots; the voice of the proletariat was not heard. Everyone was distressed by the new developments, but rats felt it the most. They could no longer peacefully enjoy the shiny trinkets they collected without paying for what was now defined as a privilege. Each one had to be declared, and applicable taxes paid in accordance with the new program.

Responding to the administrative need to enforce the various newly-established controls—in the name of public safety and well-being—Gary's cohort grew in number. Never mind that while effectuating, they were also at times executing, in a very real and permanent sense.

There was no flexibility in obeying the rules and taxes; it was do or die. Those who tried were on borrowed time, since there were a number of snitches, with eyes and ears, vying for Gary's approval; it was never long before the culprit was found out and subsequently suffered the mortal consequences.

Grumbling sustained. Winds of anger and resentment blew. Whispers of rebellion waxed vociferous. Turmoil transformed into localized battles against the cohort.

Lacking a revolutionary leader or organization, the skirmishes were as a blunt sword, unable to inflict an affecting blow.

Dewey, a mature jack opossum stepped up to fill the void.

*   *   *

Opossums are not typically known for being fighters but rather playing dead; left on their own they are fearful and avoid confrontation. Yet, when grouped together, they are fierce; their corporate teeth can make a believer out of most anyone.

Dewey, owing to his growing legion of devotees, made well-calculated attacks, only after accounting for the opposition's avoirdupois. This contributed to their success against the cohort.

*   *   *

When the masses organize against injustice, tyranny cannot prevail. It's a principle of rightness, and is integrally connected to society's perception of freedom. It's a range of freedom, certainly, and as long as things remain within that range, society can be tolerant. Push them beyond those loosely defined limits, and eventually rebellion is guaranteed.

The greed and psychopathy of Gary led him indeed to push across and beyond. Rebellion was inevitable. He was beginning to feel the push-back of a resentful proletariat.

Following months of skirmishes, loss of life, and a battle-scarred and dying cadre, some of whom went AWOL, Gary's power waned, and his wealth was nearly depleted. It was in a hollowed out tree trunk that he made his final stand.

The opossums, backed by the antlers of the deer, and the badgers with their unique flavor of vicious, saw Gary take his last breath, spelling the end of a woebegone season. Legs were given to their freedom. Sunsets seemed more beautiful, and the birds' songs more harmonious. Subsequently, things tended toward the standard of good times past.

Hope, formerly lost in a sea of disappointment, had washed ashore, once again in reach of those formerly holding it.

*   *   *

Compelled to search for their food during the cover of darkness, the badgers prefer to find and eat their food in the daylight. Understand that they tire of always having to live up to their namesake. They're all too familiar with their reputation, as in badger baiting, the badger game, and all of the idioms attributed to the badger's toughness.

During the nighttime they can eat in peace and tranquility without having to uphold their "impenetrable" facade. For these reasons they tend to live a nocturnal existence.

Small, as badgers go, at just four months Lile was already showing himself to be a precocious earthworm and rodent hunter. He gathered far more than he could use...

The Message

Perplexed by what he read, Tipee sat down on the inclined edge of the stump of a long-ago fallen tree, to consider the heinous words on the sheet of Manila paper he was served.

After sitting thoughtfully for a while, he walked home. When he got there he avoided looking at his young son and went straight to the makeshift kitchen. In robotic motion, he took an empty soda pop bottle and heated it over the single-flame propane burner.

His eyes wide but expressionless, and with sweat streaming down his face, he walked over to his curiously attentive son, held him down, pulled back the then-screaming boy's eyelid, and in one struggling motion, stuck the bottle to the child's right eye and plucked it from its socket.

It was a time of unrest, with rumblings of discontent, as one would expect under the oppressive rule of a psychopathic tyrant. Yet those discontented subjects lacked a leader—one with a vision for freedom—they were merely simple people who dreamed of it, but lacked the wherewithal to chase it down and become its master.

Freedom is that way; if you don't take it by the reins, it will run like a wild mustang, whinnying and kicking as it goes. Once forced into submission, it must be guarded so as to prevent its wandering again. Yet this, itself, is a conundrum; when compelled to guard something at the cost of that which is guarded, incremental drift carries away this already elusive and tenuously-held captive.

Then, when you're not minding it, a group or individual will say, "Here, let me watch that for you." Welcoming relief, you accept the offer and go on about what pleases you. It's a poor, but easily-kept substitute that leads down the pathway to subjugation. So goes the cycle of society.

Karphune grew up in a well-off family, by any standard. He, like his ruling father, and predecessor, was the most charming of psychopaths. As a boy, he was cruel and therefore unliked, which one could say hastened the way to his harsh, plutocratic rule. Yes, he was charming, and those with less insight, or from far-away places and therefore unfamiliar with his ways, thought him to be most pleasant. They didn't know what went on behind closed doors, if you will.

We've all read about, or even seen, rulers like Karphune—the ones who take, without giving. They often feign a personable nature. Nevertheless, their deeds may be dark and overt; no one dares whisper a word against them for fear of macabre reprisals, which can be many, varied, and grave.

His palace was richly appointed, with bounteous luxury for his enjoyment and to satisfy his want for pleasure. In contrast, the people existed in their meager surroundings, often concerned about where their next meal would come from. While he spared no expense for himself, he spared every expense for those over whom he ruled. He was an evil man to the core.

People worked, and some even worked hard, but after the tax burden was paid, little was left to allow them to engage in the comforts of life. The only reward for their labor was a ramshackle roof over their head, and basic sustenance.

The streets were dirt and sand that became pothole-ridden muck during the monsoons. For the remainder of the year there were billowing clouds of dust that would settle on the floors of their huts.

Some 30 percent of the male population of the province was blind. This worked partially in Karphune's favor, and partially against. These blind people had needs which had to be paid for by his administration. Nevertheless, they also held no threat against him, for how can a blind man fight or rebel? Neither can he effectively instigate riots. He's left to acquiesce to the leadership, and endeavor to persevere, praying his needs might be met, albeit as minimal as the government determined them to be.

You might think that Tipee was an evil man, and a horrendously sadistic father. Perhaps you are right in saying, but maybe, just maybe, he's more like you than you think. What man has not the will to survive, and see his lineage carried on, leaving a legacy to his name? And to what extremes will he go to achieve that goal? Each of you has the same drive, just as does Tipee. Yes, don't judge him, lest you judge yourself with the same sentence you expound upon him.

You see, I saw the note which caused him to sit and consider, on that stump of the long-ago fallen tree. Nay, I've seen many of them. They are horrifically etched in my mind, without hope of erasure. You must understand that I was served one as well.

It read, "Let it be known that the recipient of this legal and binding document shall present his male child possessing two eyes, to the Council of Determination for the extrication of both eyes."

Stillness, Then Terror

His body would not respond: his voice, silent.
He had only a hazy knowing...a subdued
understanding. The pounding persisted with
brief respites, only to be issued again and
again. Then it stopped; the pounding ceased.
Silence ensued. A veil of stillness consumed
him.

Moments later there began an overtone of
what sounded like murmuring. Relentlessly,
he made what were futile attempts to
animate his rigid body. His vocal cords
vetoed his attempted vociferations. How had
lethargy settled so deeply into his faculties?
Utterly helpless, he lay there.

Movement was again perceivable. Perhaps it
would incite some of his own physical
momentum, releasing his body and voice
from this insufferable enfeeblement.
However hard he tried, not so much as a
finger could he twitch. Corresponding
attempts to vocalize with all his might yielded
nary a peep. The undulations ceased, then
murmuring commenced.

His body pleaded with the blackness and cold of the apparent night to allay pervading his marrow, even his soul, though he felt it was inevitable.

Sensing his platform move again, he had a feeling of free swinging, with successive weightlessness and weightiness. Something seemed familiar, while entirely not. It continued for a few moments, and then all was still—still as before, but somehow more so—and quieter.

Murmuring ceased, or had become imperceptible. Tremendously loud rumbling and crashing sounds came rapidly, gradually becoming muffled, finally silent—complete silence in total darkness.

He lay there a moment, and then...terror struck!

Under My Bed

He's been there for such a long time. Sometimes I see him at night, slipping out from his cover, at least I think so. It could be just a shadow, but it's hard to tell for sure in the dark. Nevertheless, I know he's there.

I got the nerve to look under my bed one day, but he must have been hiding—I found nothing. When I retreated, I did so quickly because he might have otherwise grabbed me, pulling me down to torment.

He's all black, save his large, yellow-gray teeth, and a bit of white in his eyes. He's angry and full of hate. I've not seen him, exactly, but my mind is very sharp, and able to know things. Therefore, I know he's there.

He has a sort of fur, but it's smooth and plastic-like; a rubbery plastic, that is. He lies there, waiting to pounce. It's me that he wants, but for no good purpose, I'm certain. His ears, pointy; his chin, round. His body is fairly flat, which is to his virtue, as there's not much room for him beneath my bed.

The monster is an excellent hider. It's because I've looked for him but never found him, directly. Nevertheless, I know he's there.

He has no blood, or bones, like regular creatures. He's more made of quite-dense cloud-like material, that would feel solid to the touch. Maybe he's a spirit from the underworld. There's nothing good about him, or his intentions.

Whenever he's there, which is all the time, he imparts fear. I believe he especially likes ankles, though feet, I surmise, are his second favorite. He's never succeeded in getting me, though I know he has tried. I'm too clever and quick for him; he hasn't gotten ahold of me.

You have one as well, though it's possible that you don't know it. He's very quiet, even silent. But believe me, he's there.

Be clever. Be quick! You must be. You may have never seen him, but he's there.

So do you? Do you have a scary monster under your bed?

Voices

They say only crazies hear voices, but not so. We all hear them. They are the voices of the past, some are kind, some not. Whatever their message, they go with us, whispering.

Old and vagrant, the disheveled man entered the crosswalk under cover of morning darkness and ocean mist. He didn't like being seen in the daylight because the voices said so. This particular voice was more of an echo because he'd heard it so many times—all his life, really. It had become so settled in his thinking that there was no need for it to speak much, for the phantonym's message, though false, was crystal clear.

Later that day a successful businessman and community leader walked across that very same crosswalk. He however, traversed the walk in the light of day, on the way to his car—there was no inner need for him to impress anyone; he simply enjoyed the performance of a Porsche. The voices he heard were mostly echoes as well, saying little.

The voices had trained and coaxed each for years on how to think, and how to behave. Both men followed obediently: in accordance with the early-established principles initially imparted by those who mattered.

As life progressed there was little change in the comprehension of their separate echos, and each voice remained faithful until death.

Posthumously, the vagrant was processed and buried by the municipality, and promptly forgotten.

The businessman's estate paid for his well-attended wake and funeral. Many lamented his passing, and eloquent eulogies were spoken. His burial site was well-appointed within a lovely manicured backdrop. He still comes up occasionally in conversation.

The Resume

Clifton could not remember who he was.
He'd presented his resume so many times
that he lost himself within the lines of text. All
there was with which to identify himself was
what he had written on that single page,
printed one-side on high-quality white paper.

His profile was succinct and impressive; a
detail-oriented professional, his experience
was deep and wide, not specific to any field
or profession.

Lacking no assurance of his capabilities, the
man behind the resume would not suffer
disdain. Clearly a born leader and team
player, he knew how to follow instructions,
receive criticism, manage people, and be
managed: an uncompromising procession of
service and quality. A conforming non-
conformist, Clifton was agreeably
disagreeable, and suitable for any position
that pays well.

Successes included a nebulous assortment
of work-related embellishments which made

him appear to be the cohesive force behind every company for which he had worked. This is all that he could remember about himself.

An apprehensive feeling came over him; he thought that perhaps he was, in fact, no more than a physical manifestation of the resume. If so, he extrapolated, should it be lost he would also be lost in the oblivion of all things unknown or forgotten.

It followed that the sheet of paper he was holding in his hands was his nexus between identity and anonymity; between existence and empirical nonexistence. For that reason, he never went anywhere without his resume to confer, should the need arise.

The thought came to him:, what would I do if I lost it? After considering this foreboding question, realizing the conundrum, Clifton made a number of copies and squirreled them away, lest he risk also losing himself.

That resume was his security blanket, his owner's manual, his id, ego, and superego. It was his defining element, giving him the clarity to achieve his professional goals. Work was a success, which carried over to his personal life, so long as it paralleled his attributes as delineated thereon.

Clifton, by most outward appearances, remained buoyant and engaging; his resume, by definition, made him so.

Pretty Box

There are things that we know. There are things that we do not know. And there are things that we cannot know. The things we know shift and vary, as sands with the wind and waves. The things we don't know have the potential to be known, with the necessary information. The things that we cannot know, simply cannot be known.

For instance, why does a man love a woman? Why has the dog such fearless loyalty? What is that nuance of difference between a living being and a dead one? This latter set, those things which cannot be known, will remain just that, I'm quite sure.

Interestingly, we often act as though we know that which we do not. And those things that we know, we may insist to be so, regardless of any verifiable information to the contrary. Perhaps we know less than we think.

Certainly, there are far more things that we don't know than things we do. Knowing and not knowing is rather unstable ground, so watch your step.

Nevertheless, mankind tends to insist on knowing something. Therefore, he takes what he thinks he knows, what he does not know, and what he cannot know, puts them into a box, ties them up with a pretty bow, and calls it faith.

He walks about showing his pretty box, insisting that everyone join him by getting a pretty box just like his. After which warm feelings can be shared by virtue of having a common set of beliefs about things they know, things they do not know, and things they cannot know.

This attractive package surely contains the answers to all of their questions. "One must only believe!" they would say. And believe, you'd better! Those with the pretty boxes expounded all sorts of punishments that would surely befall, should you not agree that their pretty box is the most pretty.

There were other groups in town that also had pretty boxes. They looked similar, but not exactly. Conflicts were breaking out here and there when those with one pretty box came upon others with a different pretty box. An argument might ensue about whose pretty box was the prettier.

It wasn't long before there were all colors and sizes of pretty boxes. Some were bigger, and some were smaller; some were elegant, and others quite plain. Some had distinctive covers over their tops to better identify them as more special than the others.

Each group would try to persuade those with another pretty box, or no pretty box at all, to get one like theirs—they called this *sharing*.

It became commonplace to hear bickering and arguing about whose pretty box was better, or prettier, or smaller, or bigger. Many were standing at the ready to vociferate compelling arguments.

One group became militant, declaring that anyone who didn't have a pretty box like their super special pretty box was to be considered an "outcast." A few even went so far as to say that whoever did not have pretty boxes like theirs should be tortured or even killed! It frightened a lot of people who didn't have the super special pretty boxes.

Nevertheless, those with the other pretty boxes were also afraid of the punishments to be received should they forsake their own pretty box. They tried not to think about it. That worked for some.

Another group appeared on the scene, who, though small in numbers, had no pretty box whatsoever. They didn't much like any of the pretty boxes. For them to consider having one of the pretty boxes, they would need scientific evidence proving their need for one.

To this day, one can hear the ongoing bickering of the present, and the echoes of the past, never finding agreement or resolution.

History has written much about the pretty boxes, but rarely in a favorable light--perhaps it would be better if there were no pretty boxes.

Surely you have an opinion, with lots to corroborate it, including those things you know, those things you don't know, and those things you cannot know.

One Step Forward And Two Steps Back

I was reared on the canvas, weaned against the ropes. That's how it began…

There was never a time without a fight, at least not that I recall. Admittedly, the negatives can eclipse the good. When one burns their finger, say, no larger than your pinky nail, the pain is consuming, leaving no thought of the 99 and 64/100ths percent of your body that otherwise feels no pain. So yeah, it's the fights that we remember the most. That's where I've spent my life—on the canvas, up against the ropes.

My old man wasn't a part of my life. Oh, he was around, but his angry presence was something to be avoided. Surely, and within moments, what initially appeared to be a potentially pleasant encounter with him, would accelerate into a new battle in the war of existence. And that's what existence was, a war. He seemed to prefer life in the square circle. A state of conflict is where he was the most comfortable, so it seemed. My "most comfortable" was away from him, ergo, he was not a part of my life.

Perhaps, you are thinking, surely mother was there to moderate the war. The answer is a resounding no. She had her own battle to fight. However her weapons were different from mine. Mine was a strategy of avoidance; she used a more subtle form of combat, passive aggression, where a *yes*, was secretly a *no*.

Her momentum was tangibly in that direction, though the old man never seemed to notice. Alternatively, maybe he simply saw it as kicking a dead horse, or fighting with a corpse. There was no sport in it, and no feeling of overcoming the conflict.

A fighter personality needs the win, now and again, to sustain his drive. When a limp carcass is thrown into the ring, the fighter has nothing to win. The draw of the sport is in the struggle for the win, not in the winning. He simply always won with her. There was no sport to it—she entered the ring with her loss due to apparent submission. That has no appeal for a fighter.

My strategy of avoiding the ring was effective. At least until I made the second biggest mistake of my life; I got married.

It seemed like a good idea at the time. What I didn't see was the strange mix of my mother and my father in the woman. Looking back, it was likely predictable—we do tend toward the familiar.

Her usual relational strategy was passive aggression, unless I said something that brought out her inner fighter, and then she would come out swinging. She was comfortable with either role. I was comfortable with neither, but it all felt so damned familiar.

Familiarity can be a dangerous place to camp. We've all experienced doing something that's familiar.

Marketing has two main peregrine tactics: desire and familiarity. Peregrine, I say, because we are arguably not born with them, but they are instilled in us by outside forces along the pathways of life.

Most targets of advertising can be persuaded to buy something out of one of these two ethereal elicitations. With her, I bought both.

Held within the ring by the ropes, the canvas is where we lived, breathed, conversed, shared—all of which, from the outside looking in, was a continuous boxing match. Of course, the ropes were in our minds, but nevertheless, they held us within by desire and familiarity.

Life has been a pilgrimage of misdirection. A journey of one step forward and two steps back. What should look like my future, is actually my past, projecting forward.

For the first time, yesterday I got a glimpse of my future. It was unfamiliar, nevertheless, I think I desire it. I cannot say for sure, since the only perspective I've known is my past.

At least I've dipped my toe in the pool of new experiences. The reflection I saw was not crystal clear; there was a ripple of confusion, with leaves of autumn obscuring the view.

After autumn, comes winter. Yet if I follow the pattern of the fight of the seasons and renewal, spring will eventuate—a welcome consolation. As I wait for my spring, there will be work. The ropes will have to be severed. The canvas torn asunder.

Considering these necessities, glimpses of my possible future again flash in my mind. There is much work to do.

So, you ask, what was my biggest mistake? I don't know. We'll see how life goes outside of the ring...

Upside Down Smile

Huey was born to a family with a long line of backwardses, which may help explain his unusual attribute. Nurses excitedly gathered around, purportedly to see the new delivery, but their faces told a different story; more as if they were there to view a curious spectacle.

He was crying out loud like most babies do, but there was something peculiar— something surprising! You see, the postpartum crying was accompanied by a great big smile! How could such a happy baby cry up such a storm?

He looked thrilled, but sounded as angry as a storm cloud. Onlookers felt confused, not knowing if they should be happy with a smile, or feel bad with a frown. He was so crying, uh, happy!

Mother and father got ready to take Huey home. Leaving, there was no shortage of puzzled expressions following them down the corridor and out to their car.

Once home, his big hazel eyes were an invitation to tickle his tummy. Huey rewarded them with wonderful cooing sounds, as happy babies do. But that unnerving frown!

And so it went for the subsequent months; everyone made themselves too busy to visit little Huey. Perplexed, mother carried him in for a visit to Doctor Winkwink, who, after checking him, had neither diagnosis nor prognosis. Winkwink recommended that she take Huey to Doctor Nudgenudge, who specialized in happy frowns and unhappy smiles.

Following a number of tummy tickles, several funny faces, one 'boo,' a couple of scowls, and a raspberry or two, Doctor Nudgenudge conclusively diagnosed the issue: Huey's smile was upside down.

Really, it was no grand surprise. After all, his father's ears were on the wrong sides of his head, and it was mentioned that mother had her grandmother's nose! Huey's father was also known to bend over backwards to help others, and his sister Aunt Hortense surely had eyes on the back of her head. His university-professor uncle with the PhD, who had two left feet, knew almost everything forwards and backwards. So while it wasn't expected that Huey's smile would be upside down, such did seem to run in the family.

Doctor Nudgenudge suggested a minor surgical procedure. He explained how he would reverse the backwards, by switching the smile nerves with the frown nerves from the top to the bottom, and the bottom to the top, so the smile would be up and frown would be down.

He added, "The reverse of this simple procedure is normally performed on crabby old men, to help them look happier. The reviews have been marvelous!"

Everyone thought Doctor Nudgenudge's idea was brilliant; the good doctor took a moment to reflect on his intellect. "Right then, let's get on with it," he added, having finished with his introspection.

The procedure went without complication. Huey didn't seem to know the difference, but maybe, just maybe, he wondered why people stopped looking confused when he smiled, and bewildered when he cried!

With his smile thereafter working in the right direction, he lived happily ever after—as everyone could happily see!

The Misunderstood Spoon

Lying in the drawer amidst a plethora of other flatware, it found that existence had become reliably uninteresting. Everyone needs purpose.

Verbally poking, the dinner forks could be overheard gossiping about how the spoon was never used. The salad forks joined with similar prodding, but their added shortness made him more sharply feel the sting of their tines.

The knives brandished fewer words, but theirs cut deeply, provoking, albeit gently as one might expect from a spoon, his ire.

The chopsticks joined in with mutterings that he couldn't understand, but their strange words had an air of judgment. This wasn't expected since the long, slender duo themselves saw little action, and when they did, it was with children who wanted to explore playing with such unusual utensils— one or both of which would sillily end up in a child's nostril.

There was no one that the spoon could call friend. The darkness of the drawer left it feeling alone with visions of past hopes and unfulfilled expectations. It had so much to give, but was, perhaps, misunderstood. It felt alone, wondering if it would meet its demise in the box of random things, from which nothing returns.

The days of its forging were ones not unlike an awakening, when its form was created and purpose instilled. As he was heated and shaped, the fires of his awareness were lit.

It was decided by its all-knowing maker that its purpose was to be a spoon. This was perfectly fine, as he was of a gentle nature, not wanting to cut, poke, jab, or prod.

Knowing that it would always be at hand when enjoying a comforting bowl of soup, or stirring a pot of rich mushroom sauce, it savored the expectation. Its purpose was to delve into the chocolate chip mint ice cream, then lift it to please the eagerly anticipating buds.

Certainly, it is the one they would enlist to draw the delicious raspberry jam from the jar and onto the warm-buttered toast, or swirl milk and sugar into a hot cup of coffee.

Unlike the impatient forgemasters of tools, who heat their creations to a glowing red and then shock them horribly by dropping them into a cooling bath, forgemasters of flatware are a patient lot. They go about their handiwork, while waiting for the formed utensil to gently cool, before advancing to the next stage of production, or final polishing. The spoon relished the care taken in each step of its creation.

Having never had one, a happy family purchased the spoon, excitedly carried it home, and placed it on the counter, anticipating its use! Sadly, the spoon's hope of purpose was quickly dashed—eventually becoming buried by naysaying flatware. This family simply did not know how to use it.

Mother tried it for her soup, with no success. Nearly all of the scooped-up contents rolled right off the spoon. Father tried it also, with the same results. The broth and bits all instantly ran off—a frustrating encounter for all. Occasionally, a piece of vegetable would remain, but it was so inefficient that the soup would grow cold.

This, you see, is why the forlorn spoon wound up in the drawer, covered by every which and whatever kitchen utensil that was tossed in, leaving it buried, forgotten, and without hope.

The closest the sad little spoon got to food was an occasional wayward crumb, a speck of ground pepper dropped from a wildly twirled mill, or a bit of salt sprinkled by an over-eager shaker. Once a green pea rolled into the drawer and came to rest near the neck of the spoon; it eventually became dry and got knocked to a back corner, where it remains to this day.

Little Timn, who had been a baby most of his life, had advanced from pulling pots and pans out of the lower cabinets, to reaching up over the flatware drawer. Groping around, he got his hand around an unseen item—the curves of the spoon caught his tactile attention.

.

Grasping it, he studied it for a moment and then plopped it right into his mouth. Not knowing what it was for, he liked it because the cool metal made his teething feel better and wasn't pokey like forks.

Mother walked in about that time, picked him up and placed him in his high chair, for breakfast. Timn liked cereal and milk, and would dip his little hand down into the bowl to pull out a milky little handful, which mostly found its way into his mouth.

Timn grunted to his mother and reached out toward the spoon lying on the floor where he had dropped it—Mother agreeably picked it up and handed it to him. What happened next she was not expecting.

Timn buried the spoon right down into the bowl, and scooped up a sizable portion of cereal and milk! Dismayed, Mother looked down at him as he shoveled the tasty goodness into his mouth. It was at that moment that Mother realized her mistake—they had been using it upside down!

The little spoon *was* useful! They simply didn't understand it.

The spoon became one of the family's favorite utensils. It was used to slurp soup, stir the mushroom sauce, dip ice cream, scoop jam, and swirl coffee.

It was wonderful finally to be understood!

Geoff The French Lover

What began as a typical day, hanging low in a pair of dark blue, paisley-printed skivvies, was actually the beginning of a transition to self-actualization. He had never had any thoughts, whatsoever, but there was an undeniable back and forth motion of which he suddenly seemed to have some awareness. There wasn't enough information to know just what was happening, or where he was, but he liked it.

The man to whom he belonged, Geoff, thought he had a pimple, but as time passed it developed a more distinct shape. One day, as he was checking the "pimple," he realized it was looking back at him. Then it blinked. Shocked by what he saw, he tucked it back into his skivvies and apprehensively looked out the window to be sure no one saw him; he wasn't sure why.

Considering the strangeness of the occurrence, he concluded that it was no more than what he *thought* he saw, rather than what he saw. There was no tiny eyeball, just a pimple. They only persist for a few days, and then everything will be fine, he reassured himself. However, there was a nagging thought that it had indeed been there for months. Concern returned, and apprehension, and a creepy feeling, followed by more concern, more apprehension, and more creepy feelings.

Finally, it got the best of him—he had to take another look. With his head slightly cocked sideways, and his eyes in a slight squint he took another peek. No! He thought, as the eye opened again and looked back at him.

It would appear that they were at an impasse. Neither would look away, but remained with locked gaze. That's when the member spoke: "Bonjour." And that's when Geoff fell to the floor, having fainted.

Several minutes passed before Geoff became aroused, and remembered what he thought he heard. Surely, he thought, it was the wind, or...or what? Bonjour? Bonjour?! How can this be? It was all too bizarre to be true. He considered amputation, but quickly dismissed it as an impulsive and impractical idea. He couldn't think of a solution just yet, and decided to check again to see if it might have been his imagination.

He grimaced and took another peek. Geoff realized it was, in fact, just a pimple...until its eyelid opened. Smiling, it said, "Bonjour, je m'appelle Monsieur Heureux!" It was the beginning of a new relationship.

Geoff realized he would need to learn French; he obviously couldn't send his new "friend" to English class (out of modesty and attachment), so he began with the basics, "...in the privacy of your own home," as the course advert highlighted.

Geoff was surprised by how difficult French was; the verb conjugation was nearly a deal breaker. Nevertheless he pressed on, eventuating success.

The French are known for a number of social qualities. One of which is their reputation for being lovers. Geoff and his "partner," were both becoming more self-aware. Geoff, becoming more aware within the realm of love, and his partner in the realm of, well, awareness. Together, they were gaining at least this one French social quality.

Time passed. The duo grew in confidence and competence. Geoff met a girl. They liked each other. But what came of this ménage à trois, if you will? That will be a story for another day. For now, let's let it rise...naturally.

New Man

Mirrors are a loathsome thing—he knew this to be a universal truth for everyone...save just a few. For most, they're best avoided. It's unfair, Levy thought, looking at his reflection. What he saw was not what he thought he should see.

The man peering back at him looked old. Grizzly came to mind: old, grizzly. His self-image got stuck, way back when. What he expected to see lagged a couple of decades behind what he was seeing. Nevertheless, he dragged himself into bed and went to sleep. Tomorrow, however, would unfold a distinctively new day.

Morning broke quickly, and being Saturday, there was no alarm to wake him. Even so, the unwelcomed light through the edges of the blind became a lingering distraction from sleep. Joseph would be expecting him anyway, so the warm blankets would have to carry on alone.

Jammied, he walked into the bathroom, made water, then turned around to the mirror. It would be an understatement to say he was startled. He snapped his head around to see who was behind him, and by reflex looked at the edge of the mirror. Inquisitively, he laid his fingertips on the surface.

There was certainly no one else in the room so he looked again with understandable shock and curiosity; the image in the mirror was that of a different man, a much younger man, a more attractive man, someone he had never seen.

His typical morning routine was to stare at his face in the mirror, press down the wild hairs on his head with a little water, disinvite any blemishes that had popped up overnight, decide if he wanted to shave or not, pluck a few nose hairs, and wonder if he looked older than the day before. But this new image rattled his routine. Who was this man in the mirror?

Hustling down the hallway he checked the mirror in the second bathroom; it was the same stranger. All too perplexing, he went and sat in his easy chair, and hoped that afterwards, he would find himself bereft of this bizarre occurrence. Then, when he revisited the mirror, everything would be back to normal; he could shift this radical ripple in the road of his reality, to the realm of those things seen in his rear-view mirror, like roadkill run over and forgotten.

*   *   *

We've all had our personal *return to Egypt* moments, and this was one of his—reminiscing of the past, disregarding his former feelings. He downed the shot of whisky he'd left at his chair the night before.

Perhaps it was just the damn mirror. Surely it was, and the Scotch helped the thought along. He was in no hurry to find out, for some reason. Perhaps it was the whisky speaking. Perhaps it was the whisky that massaged his cynicism toward life. It seemed that no one cared about him; he'd come to not care about much of anyone, or himself.

Regret stopped in, greeting him with a sustained handshake. Mostly to remind him how insufficient he was, and what mistakes he had made to get to where he was today. The irony is that he was far more successful than regret, or himself, would ever acknowledge.

Buoying in some pointless sea of introspective retrospection, his whisky-induced buzz subsided and curiosity got the best of him. That's when he remembered that which he needed to face—his face.

Apprehensively, he walked back to the mirror, and then, half squinting, peered around the edge of the dreaded harbinger of what may come to be. Aghast, he found the same strange face. Surely, a distinctively new day was indeed unfolding. He called in sick.

*   *   *

Some say they've never been married. It's not true. Everyone marries someone or something at a young age. We're all married to what's familiar. Levy is no different. His life partner was a perception of himself, a paradigm, if you will. Every waking moment was spent with her, and at times, manifested in his dreams as well. Those dreams looked like public nakedness, or awkward embarrassment.

What Levy and many of us need is a paradigm shift—a different way of thinking about ourselves. Belief is a powerful force, and most everything will manifest in alignment to it, at least to some degree.

Levy had a way out of his paradigm, something most of us don't get.
One might say that the old rules could be tossed out; maybe this was a new beginning, though fear suggested that it might be the start of an ending: a flaming one. Would anyone know who he was? Was this an opportunity to be who he wanted?

While he felt the same on the inside, knowing he looked entirely different on the outside allowed him, perhaps, the freedom to explore what it was like to be someone else. Could he be someone of his choosing rather than a random combination of genes? It felt like two parts excitement and four parts apprehension, surely a thrill-inducing recipe.

Betraying oneself, and substituting another is not so easily done, or lived with. One has a knowing of who they are, along with their features and personality. Take out any part of that known mix, and self-betrayal clamps down like a monkey wrench.

Chapter 2

Levy couldn't remember spending so much time at home. He found it curious that the new man in the mirror was becoming somewhat familiar—in an awkward way—but had not yet shown himself to be trustworthy.

He decided, since this new guy didn't seem to be going anywhere and he really needed some groceries, to walk to the market. They knew him well enough to say hello, so it could be a way to show and tell. That is, show himself and gauge their response, or tell him something if it went sideways. He didn't know what to expect.

*   *   *

The door hinges kreened their usual welcome, the door closer gave its resistance like a zealot, and Tina, the cashier, said, "Hi Levy, haven't seen you around much lately." Surprised she recognized him, his face flushed. "Yeah, been kinda busy." Pausing, he nervously added, "I'm good," whisking a fly off of his forehead.

Collecting one of their tiny red shopping carts, he shuffled through the aisles, gathering groceries, while watching and being wary along the way.

Levy wanted to get out of there quickly so he didn't buy much. Checkout would have gone quickly if Tina wasn't so talkative. People liked her for that quality. Nevertheless, today he only nodded politely, gave some acknowledging grunts, paid for what he got, whisked the fly off his forehead again and himself out the door.

Out of vacation days, Levy decided to try going back to work...see how it would go. Strange things began to happen. People recognized him like nothing had changed. Confused, he jokingly thought to himself how this situation gave a whole new meaning to knowing "the man in the mirror."

Days passed, and with that, confidence grew. His interactions improved. Others started asking for his thoughts on their work; socratically, he let them find their own answer, without him working to get it, or telling them what to do.

When the section manager position opened, he was all-in, coasting into it like destiny was a long, gentle slope. Not long afterward, was when it happened.

Chapter 3

Mirrors didn't mean much to him any more— he could take them or leave them.

Morning broke quickly, and being Saturday, there was no alarm to wake him. Even so, the unwelcomed light through the edges of the blind became a distraction from sleep. Joseph would be expecting him anyway, so the warm blankets would have to carry on alone.

Jammied, he walked into the bathroom, made water, then turned around to the mirror. It would be an understatement to say he was startled. He snapped his head around to see who was behind him, and by reflex looked at the edge of the mirror, then inquisitively laid his fingertips on the surface. He was back.

He didn't know how or why, but seeing his old self didn't bother him like it used to. The grizzly man in the mirror looked like an old friend—one he had missed, at that. He laughed. He laughed and smiled at himself. It was a new day, and that with an old friend. It was going to be okay, no matter who was looking back at him.

*   *   *

Our own man in the mirror changes over time; it's true for us all. There's no getting around that, as it's part of the cycle of life. What we believe is always our truth, our reality. The interesting part of it is, we can believe what we like.

Belief need not be based on truth, but simply believed, making it our reality.

Levy had learned something through this bizarre experience. Though he was not entirely sure what it was, if he had to give some answer, it would be to believe. Believe in your goodness, in the goodness of others, and in the goodness all around you, but mostly, believe in yourself.

The Woman With Six and A Half Foot Feet

Juicy was mostly known for two things, her name and how fast she could walk. Her given name was Justine Endeavor; chosen by her father because, "A name that speaks is best for a lassie." Nevertheless, somewhere along the early part of her thirty-two years of life, a neighbor, James Ray—a crusty old farmer who always wore a brown plaid flannel shirt and a sun-bleached baseball cap—spontaneously and without deference, gave her that epithet. To her father's chagrin, it stuck.

Regarding her rapidity of ambulation, well, no one can be credited with that, as it was the direct result of a particular feature that she uniquely possessed, with which she was born. Juicy, you must understand, had 6-½ foot feet. Why, she could stuff a basketball with her big toe, and that without jumping.

During the last term of gestation, Gina, her mother, became troubled because of the power-packed kicks the baby was delivering.

The doctor assured her that it was fine and that some babies are more energetic than others, adding, "Some of the greatest movers and shakers of society were lively kickers!" "Not to worry," Doctor Haugh interjected as he left the examination room.

The fancy footwork continued, making the end of Gina's gestation a welcomed day. As is typical at birth, Justine Endeavor's head appeared first. When her feet began to follow, everyone's eyes were wide and faces surprised! This was, perhaps, the longest birth in all of history—her feet kept coming, and coming, and coming, and yes, coming. Finally, after a long-pregnant pause, out popped the toes.

All members of the birthing team were astounded...and silent. They simply didn't know what to say. Doctor Haugh regained his presence of mind, and said, "Congratulations, Gina, you have a, uh, baby girl." It was her feet that caught everyone's attention—they were huge!

News of the tyke's unusual feature quickly spread, far and wide. The whelp became rather a celebrity at her tender age, those superbly-large feet enthralling much of the world.

Talk shows, radio interviews, online platforms, were all bidding for her time. Justine Endeavor found her introduction to life a bit curious, but Gina had mixed feelings. On one hand she reveled in Justine's acclaim, but finding some peace and privacy was challenging. The incessant ringing of the phone and knocks at the door were wearying.

Nevertheless, the girl grew, and grew, as did her feet—and celebrity. More and more, they were becoming a beautiful sight to behold.

Size matters, particularly when it more easily reveals the structural nuances and beauty of the object—in this case, the feet. The juxtaposition of the phalanges and the metatarsals was exquisite. But not so much as to be eclipsed by the art nouveau-like curvature of the arch, which was given sound structure by the cuneiform and navicular. Even the calcaneus added its contribution to the sweet balance of the exceptionally pronounced podiatric pair.

Sometime after her 14th birthday, she was contacted by a certain Amadeo Agostini Argento, a board member of an international shoe company based in Italy with a collection of offices around the world. He had heard of the young woman and persuaded his company to study the feasibility of bringing Justine onboard as their iconic foot model. "Her exquisite feet," he explained, "are the perfect pair to exhibit our shoes."

Anticipating a response to the affirmative, the R&D department had been designing and producing various large-sized versions of their more popular styles—ones that, incidentally, were her size.

Dressed in his brown, Italian two-button suit and white shirt, with a red argyle tie, Amadeo knocked on the door of their modest home. Gina, trying to feel relaxed, invited him in, with a crack in her voice. She introduced Juicy, and nervously offered him coffee or tea. "Coffee, please," he replied. Juicy complimented him on his tie, and invited him to sit down while her mother made it ready. Accepting the invitation, Amadeo unbuttoned his jacket and sat down on the well-worn couch. The foam in the cushion had lost its resilience, so he sank down lower than expected.

Being Italian, his acceptance of coffee was purely a friendly gesture, since he had come to believe Americans don't understand coffee, nor are they able to make a good cup. Italians muse about Americans and their abysmally huge cups; in Italy, coffee or espresso comes in a demitasse, and is dark and flavorful.

Gina and Juicy liked Mr. Argento, and he was rather charmed by their unsophistication—the couch notwithstanding.

Getting to the details, he presented the marketing concept to Juicy and her mother, emphasizing the flexibility and minimal time commitment expected, in consideration of her tender age. Mr. Argento explained how it could be a foot in the door of success for Juicy.

They agreed that, for their convenience, twice a month the company's suiter and photography team would set up in a studio nearby. "It shouldn't take more than two to three hours," Mr. Argento, with his heavy Italian accent, assured them. Smiling, he added, "It should make only a small footprint of time in your life."

Though Argento's company wanted to sign a contract for the "ongoing and exclusive" right to Justine's feet, she and her mother felt that Justine should have her *own* ongoing and exclusive right to them. Not wanting to make a stink, Mister Argento conceded, and departed with the endorsed agreement containing the altered stipulations.

Justine put her best foot forward. Before long, however, she was out of the pot and into the fire. Shortly after the inception of the shoe company's marketing program, her feet were literally everywhere—billboards, magazines, shoe store windows, and the topic on the lips of every Tom, Dick, and Harry, and their wives, cousins, in-laws, neighbors, and strangers.

What was previously an annoyance, became an all-out assault on their sense and sensibility. Many, they discovered, were without an understanding of propriety, stepping on their proverbial toes with every stride.

When you are the only one in the world with 6-½ foot feet, obscurity vanishes. Strangers would pound on their door, day and night, asking to see and even touch them.

Reality was kicking down the door of their privacy. Juicy could go nowhere without being trampled by fans wanting pictures, autographs, and to behold her gigantic feet.

Paparazzi were merciless, constantly tracking her every step. They reliably gathered on the sidewalk outside their home, cameras flashing with any indication of movement.

Gina hired a contractor to install a 6-½' fence around their home, but construction was halted by The City for violating building code: "No fence over three feet in height shall be placed across the street side of any residential property."

Now seventeen, Juicy was becoming a young woman; she found her rockstar status to be exciting. There was, however, a downside to fame and fortune. There were more shoe companies, more contracts, more photographers, and ever more invasions of privacy than she ever would have imagined in her wildest fame-fantasy. Their home was becoming over-run with shoes— given in hopes that she would wear them for brand exposure.

Learning now what a can of worms they had opened by inviting a 6-½ inch pile of documents for the rights to her 6-½ foot feet, they tried speaking with Argento and the other shoe company representatives, requesting to be released from the feet contracts—at least for a time. All explained that she was special, having shoes that no other could fill.

She would be required to uphold her agreements; her feet were legally bound.

Gina resolved that another solution would need to be found.

It became apparent that they would have to adjust their living situation. But, wherever they would go, how does one hide such a conspicuous feature? With eleventy thousand signs and billboards of her feet—in just their town alone—realistically, there was no hope of escape.

They looked at a number of new homes in their preferred parts of town before finding one they liked. After signing another 6-½ inch pile of agreements, disclosures, and contracts, they settled into what would be their sanctuary. The centrally positioned residence was encompassed by three full acres, with an 8 foot perimeter wall, and an automatic wrought iron access gate.

Chapter 2

Youth is an exciting time, when all of the elements are present to build a solid individual. For Justine, many of these elements, though present, were eclipsed by the potentially dark cloud of fame.

It started with smoking; first she tried salmon filets and chicken breast in a Little Chief Smoker. That seemed innocent enough, but they led to jerky, baby back ribs, and eventually oxtails, in a deluxe digital patio smoker and bbq. Gina accessed a good counselor to help her daughter to get through such challenging times. The emotional havoc wreaked upon the girl, in conjunction with her aversion to control, led her to smoking the hard stuff, like gouda, gruyère, and even parmigiana.

One might expect smoking to become intertwined with drinking. It did, and similarly progressed from gateway drinks like orange juice and coconut water, to matcha green tea lattés, and the likes of double-shot espresso macchiatos.

Gina fought a growing distrust and loss of control of Justine. Juicy felt Gina was becoming more controlling. They both felt out of control. The conflict subsequently manifested in her foot care: skipping pedicures and going barefoot. This did not bode well.

Although each company's makeup artist attended every photo shoot—treating her feet so as to achieve a flawless look—regular pedicures were, according to the contracts, required and non-negotiable. Predictably, the attorneys representing the shoe companies sued for nonfeasance.

The smoking and drinking continued, while Juicy found herself in court, accused and convicted, and at the mercy of the Judge. She tried to change, but ultimately did not. Drawn to cute young men, and her vices, Justine lost her footing, sinking deeper into the mire of breaking bad.

While her feet were previously seen everywhere in a positive and beautiful light, she now joined the ranks of the dramatic— the tabloids offering top dollar for gossip and photos of Juicy, her feet, and her bare-footed companions. Rag covers were going front page with images of her calloused and dirty dogs.

What was formerly admiration, was now contempt, and displayed man's inclination for kicking them while they're down, or seeing the dirt, if you will. Their shallowness became another source of resentment for Juicy, feeling lost and confused.

Failure to care for her feet became a passive-aggressive way of answering the expectations and dominion of the corporate shoe world, toward which she had gained such disdain. They reflected how she felt. It was a response to her aversion to it all. In effect, she was saying, "You want these feet? Go ahead, but it'll be on my terms, not yours!"

Basking in the light of admiration, and the accompanying money, can grab just about anyone who's not completely sure-footed in who they are and in what they believe. Their *who* and their *what* has to be set, with clear understanding. Otherwise, one can be blown by the gale winds of pleasing others, and outside control. One's ship of identity can falter or be lost on far-off and unknown horizons. Justine Endeavor found herself bobbing and fearful in those distant waters, with no one to throw a life ring.

One morning Juicy found herself lying face-down in a plate of smoked squab. Her efforts to take back control became nothing more than a transfer of power, from her mother, to corporate entities, and substances. The smoking and drinking were her new masters; it was an epiphanic moment.

Chapter 3

Justine was a smart girl. She got cleaned up, dressed, put on a pair of shoes, and went out for a pedicure. She felt much better, but was emotionally exhausted, having come out of a relatively long period of passive-aggressive rebellion.

Back home, she cried for the relief she was feeling, and was pleased with herself for making personal adjustments. Juicy laid herself down on the couch and shortly fell asleep.

She dreamt of fairies scattering pixie dust over her feet, driving monster trucks with plenty of foot space and liking it, barefoot waterskiing in the boundary waters, slow dancing with Paul Bunyan, and twirling with Guanyin. When she awoke, peacefulness rested within.

*   *   *

Though Gina had been wrestling with some resentment toward Justine, the joy of seeing her standing at the front door, shadowed every negative feeling she had unsuccessfully tried not to entertain. They both cried and held each other for several minutes, making up for lost time.

Juicy conveyed a new and more positive attitude with the shoe companies, apologizing for her failure and their misfortune. Mostly, they were understanding, with a couple of exceptions, and allowed her to return and finish out her contracts.

People can be forgiving, as was the case toward Juicy. Her feet didn't have quite the value they once had, but there are always those looking for drama en lieu of harmony.

Though she kept up her foot modeling commitments, she also found time for a man, and her own family. One of her favorite sounds was the pitter patter of LITTLE feet! Little Gina, named after her grandmother, loved to stand on her mama's very large feet, and they would dance.

A Day In The Life

The man whom they served had been missing for six hours. There was something familiar to them about that, but thinking only in the moment can have its downside. Nevertheless, the way one is—their way, their personality—tends to be a constant.

There was much worry, and more argument about the *where* and *why* of his absence, including who was at fault. He was there, and then he wasn't.

Knowledge of his whereabouts, what the future would hold, or the meaning of the future, was an unknown. Even the past was but an ethereal synaptic flash—everything was simply moment by moment.

The smoke sensor was the first to voice his uniquely incessant concern. This in turn, triggered the onion's lamentation; tearfully he expressed his feelings of hopelessness, saying, "All is lost, all is lost." Wanting to comfort, the facial tissue availed itself to dab his cheeks.

Having a chip on their shoulders, the cookies' indifference was apparent. They simply asked for more milk.

Many of them didn't understand the gravity of the situation, so the brush painted a clear picture.

Volume 11 of the encyclopedias brought knowledge into the conversation, but what he said lacked wisdom.

The pencil drew analogies, however nothing was to the point; it wound up in a drawer of rubber bands, random papers, and other stuff, sequestered from further illustrations.

The soda's bubbly personality, unfortunately, was all bottled up, so no one knew.

The porch roof column was always supportive and reliable; despite that, he had a great burden, from which he could not be distracted.

The garden ornament, despite looking wind-blown and disheveled, chimed in, as everyone expected.

Predictably transparent, the open window said, "I'm feeling insecure."

Still crying, the onion uttered something indiscernible.

Garlic, as usual, said something offensive— no one likes to get too close to it.

A tree in the backyard, right outside of the unsecured window, encouraged all to stand strong; to which, the cabinet shelves added their support.

The walls, in accordance with their two-sided nature, took both sides of the discussion.

The rock was silent; perhaps he was sleeping.

The bickering continued, partially due to the tire's circular reasoning.

A donut seemed persuasive, but in essence, there was a hole in its argument—perhaps it found the coffee distracting.

There are always those who are disagreeable—the tough guys. This was no exception, and the jerky made it clear that he didn't need anyone. Noticing that the easily-provoked smoked meat strip might need his space, the door made a way out.

Getting the scoop so as to report to those interested, the spoon listened carefully, without making any personal judgements. It felt that information should come in a well-rounded serving.

For those who tended to worry, the couch throw was quick to comfort.

All the while, the backpack was getting carried away.

As the conversation was delving into the unclear and unknown, the knife cut through the contentions of a more speculative nature.

That's when the winter parka joined and things got heated; followed shortly by the chafing dish, which ultimately had everyone steamed.

Thank goodness, the ice cubes clinked in, cooling down the incensed participants.

A sentence wanted to be part of the banter, but when given the chance, his droning, run-on lines left the others bored.

Fortunately, a red marker rolled out and did some quick editing, improving the sentence's structure and thereby, readability.

Once they were quieted from arguing, the rug had the floor, but yielded to the bag who carried the conversation, until unexpectedly, the man walked back in from work.

All of the items were suddenly content and therefore silent, save the open window, who seemed to say, "Would someone please fix my latch?"

Countdown

Crossing the isthmus from this life to the unknown beyond, he intended to lay claim to every drop of life-imbuing sensation that he could; he was determined to leave that proverbial bosom of experience dry.

The first step was one he'd made before, so there was little apprehension, just the usual anticipation, albeit subdued. Nevertheless, if you knew him well, you'd say he looked half-crazed and was going off half-cocked. There was a twinkle in his eyes that suggested he was about to put one over on fate.

Momentarily, he could hear the sound of the passing air, and feel the exhilaration of the emotional rush. All that was familiar to him was distant, barely visible. It was as though an unseen ant colony with, to an outside viewer, no defined purpose, but nevertheless there, animated by something unknown or internal. He remembered the ant farm he had as a child. Below him were farmhouses, barns, and rectangular plots of land. The "ants" were there, but not easily seen at his altitude. An existential awareness came over him—he nodded side-to-side and gave a short breath-laugh.

Rolling over onto his back, he simultaneously felt fear and exhilaration; having trained himself to subdue the first, he reveled in the second. The air had a light fragrance of ozone; he inhaled deeply. All of his senses were reporting for duty—sensations he lived for.

A quick gyration had him prone. Past most of the cloud cover, he could better take in the splendid view. His mind went blank as he scanned the field of view.

He remembered a favorite movie as a kid, Parachute Battalion, and Private Bill Burke, who was his inspiration. Like Private Burke, he too was terrified of his initial plunge, and recalled crying in helpless fear before being forced out of what was supposed to be a tap-out jump. Nostalgically, he grinned.

Britches, his childhood dog, whose namesake was derived from the pattern of his coat, brought a tear to his eyes as he reminisced. Britches spent most of the years in his young master's heart, having been run over by a car while chasing after a taunting squirrel.

At 2500 feet he instinctively reached for his ripcord, then remembered—there wasn't one. He rolled onto his back again.

Considering his plan, one last time, his thoughts turned to his late mother and wife. Having lost them both was beyond devastating, so in those final seconds, he alternately spoke the names of those that meant the most to him, "Mother...Laura... Mother...Laura...Mother...Laura…Muh"

Neat And Tidy

Setting down his lunch bag on the counter, Toffler swung open the fridge door and grabbed an ice-cold Genesee. It's not that it was his favorite beer, but at 99 cents for 24 ounces, it feigned his favorite, and had done so since he started his job so many years ago. His eyes went up toward the ceiling as he did some quick math. "31 years!" he exclaimed, mildly aghast. Day in, day out, the same ten weekday hours with overtime.

Toffler was actually his family name, but its emergence as a moniker is traced back to the inspiration and repetitious use by his Pint-Sized Football League (PSFL) coach, who ironically was also pint-sized. His years around Coach, playing on the PSFL, caused it to stick, ergo, he was Toffler to everyone who knew him.

Sipping on his beer, he reflected on what he suspected about the ten hour days with overtime, surmising that it was the factory's way of getting more work out of workers for the same money. They made it sound like they were doing them a favor. Nevertheless, the work was okay, and he didn't have to think much about it, so his mind could wander.

Over the years, where it wandered began to change, even more so lately. Heretofore, it wandered around the trails of weekend planning, as in what he would do, or not do. Now, he found it wandering through the ruts of finding meaning in life, and what mark he would leave. Would anyone miss him if he was gone? It ambled into the inane tall grass of wondering who would come to his funeral. Not that he was expecting one anytime soon. It seemed like a concern, but silly at the same time, considering his supposed future posthumous state.

He didn't mind the work. It was something to do in his otherwise seemingly casual existence. He'd never before admitted to the emptiness of his life. Although he resisted the likes of such thoughts, it was still coming into his awareness, therefore providing additional mental real estate for his mind to further *wander*.

Arriving at the bottom of his beer, almost by reflex he walked to the freezer, pulled out a box of Banquet chicken, popped a half dozen pieces into the oven and set the timer. Sometimes he thought about having a vegetable; typically he had none, so typically he didn't. While waiting for his chicken, he turned on the TV.

Reruns of *Friends* would be on right about now, so he pulled the trigger on that. Commercials were running; he didn't mind—and watched them with about the same regard as the regularly scheduled programming.

We all have our share of the scars brought on by life, or other people...even lovers. His biggest scar looked like a girl. Blonde, slender, white-toothy smile, and legs for days—the Rembrandt of women, if you will. Oh yeah, she was easy on the eyes, but hard on the psyche.

Just out of high school he married who would become his permanent scar; it was short-lived. After the divorce, which was easy since it was uncontested and they had nothing of any real value, he decided the motivation for tying the knot was postpartum depression—parting from the sociality of so-called academia.

She succinctly, albeit insensitively, clarified how she felt about him with her valedictory comment, "Loser, l-o-o-s-e-r," slamming the door behind her.

At that moment, she thought about leaving the door open disrespectfully for him to close, but her temper got the best of the situation; the whole house shuddered. By then there was no love lost.

He knew he wasn't the sharpest tool in the shed, but he did know how to spell loser; though he did check it on his phone to be sure—he triumphantly smiled when it confirmed that he was right.

Occasionally they pass on the street, where without exception, he looks dumbfounded, and she purses her lips in contempt; he suspects she discovered her spelling error.

Since the divorce he dated a number of times, but that word loser kept reverberating in his head. He didn't want to hear that from a woman again, ever, however it was spelled. Besides, what he really wanted to do was drink beer with his buddies, and get laid once a week, or preferably once a day; he felt lucky if it was once a week.

His problem with being called a loser was that he believed it—he believed it already. Melancholy came over him as he thought about it; the beer wasn't helping the matter. Never again would he be part and parcel to such a label.

What perplexed him was that he did what he was taught in the public system of subjugation—oops, Freudian slip there—that should have been *education*: be quiet and pay attention, hold still, don't rock the boat, do what you're told, don't think independently, be like others, be a pleaser. These, purportedly, were the essential steps on the pathway to success. Was it really so neat and tidy?

He wondered if this really was the pathway to success, because he didn't feel successful; and that fact was decisively corroborated by the coquettish marriage-breaker who left him. A tear came to his eye as he popped another Genesee; he could tell it was going to be a several-beer evening.

Toffler was at a crossroads, but had no idea which way to go—a veritable conundrum. So, he pulled up a metaphoric easy chair, and spent the next few years at that crossroads, reclining in comfort.

Mornings would find him fumbling for the alarm clock, crawling out of bed, walking into the bathroom, and looking into the mirror. He could see the lines of age. His eyes were beginning to have a sunken look.

The perplexity through the years was manifesting in an aged look. And not just from time, but time coupled with the burdensome things of life. The hopes he had as a young man had withered away to...somewhere...somewhere.

On one of those beset mornings he asked himself, what about love? What had he missed? Is this success? Disillusionment flooded his soul. "Know thyself. What does that really mean?" he asked the air, or someone or thing that might be listening and able to offer an answer. It fell on deaf ears, he decided; no burning bush experience for him. It was raining so maybe his bush was too wet to catch fire.

One thing was sure, he was pissed that he had been misled so many years prior. Perhaps they, then, were as confused as he was now. The blind leading the blind...typical, he thought.

Retirement years were upon him; he "didn't even get a goddamn watch." Discontent and boredom were knocking at his lonely door.

Television and leaning on a bottle reflected the final outcome of his "success." It had passed so quickly, and looking back, it was empty. Holding a visceral loathing of those who had misled him, he sunk into a torpid funk.

His appetite lost and thoughts irascible, despair was now his cellmate. Perhaps, he thought, fate established before his birth that he was born for others to break his heart. "Fate, you're a bastard," he spoke out loud.

It was a glorious day for a funeral. The sun rose, snapping the chill out of the spring morning air. Birds were singing in the trees, like the days before, and eternity past. No one came, save the ceremony conductor, of course. A lone, brown, short-haired dog trotted past to some unknown destination.

With the end of the ceremony, the gravediggers back filled and set the tombstone. Having finished the job, and a couple more, they called it a day, and went home and had a beer...and some chicken. It was all so neat, and tidy.

Floyd: A Case Study

Floyd had a large circle of acquaintances, including himself, none of whom he really knew. They were all simply part of his ongoing search for safety. Nothing else mattered to him.

It was his identity, his meaning. What he did was who he was; there was nothing deeper than his need to be safe. His person was no more than a persona, and what he did was wholly the manifestation of that persona. Long-since forgotten, his introverted nature was displaced by a facade of extroversion, his patron saint of safety.

To those around him, Floyd seemed a pleasant enough chap. The more discerning, however, were left with a thought-bubble question mark after talking with him. What it was, wasn't clear, but for those who took the time to try and understand, he seemed like a small boat in a big ocean, bobbing and rocked at the whim of a swell: a snowflake in a blizzard, unable to choose its direction, blown with caprice by popular winds.

Few spent much time thinking about it, yet somehow he had become a part of the social landscape, but no one knew why. He wasn't ignored, neither adored: an ambiguous one of the many. Not interesting enough to be enigmatic, just there. Nor did anyone miss him in his absence.

Floyd was not impressive, not so much liked, and rarely thought about. He was nothing more than a crumb, say, in the toaster of social intercourse: in that catch tray full of crumbs at the bottom that we mostly ignore.

Floyd, ironically, was entirely oblivious to what anyone thought of him. He neither considered himself enigmatic nor ambiguous. When you get right down to it, he wasn't trying to be something, or anything—just safe.

In order to want to be something, one must have a starting point. For him it would be knowing himself, but that didn't cross his mind. He didn't have so much as an inkling that he had the potential to be a unique human being.

Everything known and unknown about Floyd amounted to a shallow mire of inconsequential muck. Most of us avoid muck, unless of course, you're five and just got a new pair of "big boy" boots. (That just made you smile because you remember yours...and the muck!)

He was never able to get deep into himself, which left him shallow and clean-booted. There was a reason for this.

Cue the violins if you like, but a solid upbringing was not to be found in his formative years. There was no secure mother or strong-reliable father. She was a contemptible, abomination of a woman, consumed with herself, her opinions, and social media—a veritable narcissist.

His father was a critical rageaholic bastard who lived a plethora of reasons to be critical of himself, but wasn't—at least not to which he would admit. He saved that for Floyd, at least until the whiskey killed him.

When you cut away all of the parental facades, the boy was a product of familial dysfunction to the nth degree. That upbringing manifested in the lad; he was fraught with fears, and laden with tears—not the ideal environment for rearing a healthy child.

As far as anyone in his circle knew, he was a nobody; Floyd didn't have an opinion on it. He simply kept busy staying safe, staying secure, nothing more, nothing less, living in a constant state of arousal—the introvert from within subconsciously acting as the extrovert.

He was the small fish glomming to the aquatic wriggling mass, as they synchronously whirled in random swirls, hoping to confuse predators, thereby abating sudden inter-gastric demise.

Never known to get angry, Floyd suppressed all such feelings because he had grown up with an angry man, around whom expressing feelings was dicey at best, and usually downright unsafe. He had become sure that there was absolutely no good place for anger, and decided to resolutely stand against it. This naturally came across as a weakness.

You've heard the idiom, "Nice guys finish last." In society nice guys garner contempt, not respect; the collective tends to abhor weakness. The animal kingdom is rife with similar examples. The weak die from predation or intraspecies elimination, posthumously strengthening the whole. People are generally a little more civilized, consequently accepting the nice guys and tolerating the weak. Being tolerated was apparently Floyd's lot in life.

His ideology of safety was what he believed and how he lived. When one's ideology becomes their guiding principle, they unavoidably close themselves off from growth. You've spoken with those who are so set in their beliefs that no amount of facts or information to the contrary could change their mind. They may have even become notably agitated.

What we have and how we live has more to do with what we believe about ourselves than what or who we believe in; each element of one's dance with perspective is a lesser fractal of the overall belief system.

However deep you go in the fractals of thoughts, each is assuaged by the next.

This, my friends, is where Floyd remained until reaching his final moment, his consummate life search for safety, that hintermost breath before the locus where he and the ethereal Avalon would become one.

Aurelia's Story

Aurelia hung from her canons, yoked within her custom-built bell tower. Two cubits across, she was cast in place then hoisted to her white-washed perch under the black-slate-roofed belfry. True in both sound and deportment, she rested until the bell ringer beckoned, or was animated by the persuasive bellows of a westerly gust.

Some decades after the bell's installment, an overzealous bell ringer polished her, yielding a bright gold-hued finish—which became her namesake. Time and weather returned the bell to a dark bronze patina, though the moniker remained.

Sadly, before completing the polishing, his makeshift scaffolding collapsed. The result was a broken ankle—subsequently yielding a permanent, one-sided favoring to his walk. Nevertheless, his mark was made through this epithetic legacy. Men still speak of the foolish bell ringer, albeit with affection.

Daily the bell would toll, chiming midday, which lent regularity and a comfort-imparting rapport with the community.

What was unknown to most was that she possessed a story. It was a story of her copper-tin alloy origins brought forth by a life-long labor of devotion; the legacy of which the master bell founder cast that day after painstaking thought, planning, and preparation.

She was the eminent and, incidentally, final achievement of the aged man who had given his life over to the perfection of his craft. After the decrepit bell founder supervised its lifting into place, the bell ringer tolled announcing both its arrival, and, ironically, the sudden death of he that labored her into existence.

His last resting place was in the small cemetery adjacent to the belfry, within view and earshot of his pièce de résistance. The bell and the gravestone both stand to this day.

The Unwelcome Visitor

Laying his hand on her forehead he was shaken by her nearness to the veil that separates life from death. There he wept, finally gaining a cohesive deliverance from something that had been no more than a nebulous paradox; he realized that he loved her.

Events of time carve deeply at the soul, as if a sculptor tilling away the superfluous to reveal what lies below.

Death is an unknown; loss can afflict us acutely, and the pathway of mourning is rained with tears.

Tears cleanse as the saline rivulets percolate down, bathing the cheeks, leaving a briny crystalline residue, preserving for what lies ahead, be it joy of the heart, or midnight of the soul.

They had shared experiences, possessions, and celebrated the pregnancy that was now threatening her life. There's a twisted irony in losing one's life to begin that of another.

*   *   *

Death is an irreverent coward. When has Death looked someone squarely in the eyes before taking them to whatever lies beyond? Who has seen as much as a wisp of his shadow? What consequences befall him when determining erroneously that it's someone's time to go? This condescending poltergeist going about killing—with impunity—violates all that is good and right.

*   *   *

Those were his thoughts. He wanted to say them—scream them from a mountaintop; but he suffered that his angry decrying would evanesce, as smoke from the flame of a match.

Who could blame him, as this was not his first visit from the grim reaper. His father had been taken, his childhood friend Randy, and his old friend Earl, whom he lost after a protracted battle with illness. All were gone. There are more, but that's the short list.

Here she lay, post-op, weak. He wondered how this joyous occasion could become nothing more than a struggle to fend off Death. The procedure began her tenuous recovery.

Having made a premature visit, Death would leave empty-handed. She would remain with the living.

Her near-death experience became his rebirth. She was now much more than his partner; from that event forward, she would be his cherished bride. Was it the same for her—was love also no more than something misunderstood? He wanted to know right then; it would be some time. Issues and events of life sometimes require waiting.

Love came out of nowhere, you might think. The truth is, it came out of a hidden place; it came out of a place that's intangible. You see, it came out of the pain of potential loss. In a sense it can be seen, but more so, it's felt.

As the 'song' called life plays on, there is a descant of harmony in the nexus between the heart and the intimate relationship with another.

Today, he heard that harmony for the first time.

Never Born—A play of sorts

A woman walks into a Managed Motherhood
Clinic and desperately explains her plight.
They've heard it before; it's routine. They
lead her to a room. Lying on a gurney, she
can hear a heartbeat, but is sure it's not hers.
She looks around the dimly lit room, as
though it were a dream...all black and white.
Suddenly, there's a young man looking at
her.
He tearfully petitions, "Please reconsider".
She looks at him, but the words evade her.
Again he pleads, "Give me a chance".
She says remorsefully, "I'm sorry. I wasn't
ready for you. I didn't mean to..." her voice
trailing off.
He protested, "But why am I your decision,
and not mine?"
Emotion building, he adds, "I don't want to
die."
Painful silence permeates the room for a few
moments.
A shadowy young girl passes through the
room, jumping rope and singing Ring Around
the Roses. Pausing, she senses the gravity
of the moment.

He beseeches once more, "What will happen
to her? My daughter."
The girl frightfully scurries away.
He repeats, "What will happen to her?"
The woman then says, "I'm so sorry."
He says "I love her...my daughter.
Don't...please."
She mournfully interjects, "I'm sorry, it's too
late, it's already done." Sobbing, she closes
her eyes and turns away in shame.

His image fades away. The woman lies there
bewailing what she had done.

I was never born.
I missed all of life.
From my mother's womb, torn.
Mother, forsaken wife.

Where is my joy?
Where is my chance?
With a girl should a boy,
have nary a dance?

Let me be, let me grow.
Let me love, let me feel.
I hear my blood flow.
Let me live, I appeal.

Heart rate increases.

(whispering)
It's growing dark, hold me tight!
Oh the pain, and from where? (the heart rate elevates)
Can you not see my plight?
Can you, my life spare?

Heart rate steadily increases.

Dimmer, and dimmer grows my awareness.
What's that cold that surrounds me?
What's this stark unfairness?
I've been cast out, as if debris.

Heart rate pounds!

Goodbye mother.
Goodbye to all I would have known.
No strength left in my bones….
Heart rate flatlines.

I was never born.

Shorter Stories Begin Here

Crash

Life, as it were, seemed to be a never-ending series of crashes, although he had survived everything so far—not just fender benders. The number of head-on collisions he'd endured was more than he could count on two hands.

On a first-name basis with his prosthetist, his legs worked well. In fact, he felt as mobile as he ever did with his "original equipment," if you will. Naturally, he has the typical scars and such from being patched up so many times, but he's still able to go to work and do his job. One consolation is that he enjoys it; one could even say he's made for it.

Based on past experience, he has no expectations of spending the balance of his days crash-free. The irony, perhaps, is that in each crash, he had only driven a short distance.

At this point, he doesn't understand it, but he expects it. It's simply the way of things when you're...a crash test dummy.

Sand God

Sand, the omnipotent dictator of all things pertaining to the length of one's mortal existence, declares, one grain at a time, the approach of a man's inevitable end, to be determined by the number of grains foreordained sometime around their birth, and encapsulated within the consecrated carrier, the hourglass.

Woman In The West of Iceland

There's a woman in the west of Iceland, in the land of Grundarfjörður and Kirkjufell Mountain, who brazenly wraps her wet arms about you as you stand in awe. She's a wild one, with not a tittle of shy, and lo, drinking a glass of rye—as witnessed by her erratic pathway to the Greenland Sea.

Beginning on the land where the lubbers lie, drawing their attention to her offered affections, she slips off into the depths, becoming one with the watery world beyond the pebbly coast, where her true loyalties lie, and her lover cannot follow.

She's fickle, inattentive, and true to none—a love but feigned. She comes and leaves again, on the wings of a whirlwind.

Thorn In My Heart

She plunged a thorn into my heart.
She withdrew it with apologies; I forgave.
My heart seemed blind; it barely perceived.
Nevertheless my eyes took note; tears ran
down and healed the wound.

The Ancient Friend

Ancient stuff is of what he's made. Though immobile, this jolly old character entertained children for hours. They giggled at his pointy nose and beady eyes. It didn't bother him, rather he enjoyed the attention. Their smiles and bright eyes tickled him.

In the intervals between their visits, time seemed to stand still. On sunny days, when most others were exhilarating in the warm rays, tears, as it were, ran down his face.

He could feel that the end of his time was drawing near, yet joyfully he remained, knowing that he would again return, perhaps next winter. Soon, he would be all but forgotten—nothing more than a vague, albeit lingering memory in the minds of the children.

The puddle inevitably dissipated, leaving behind a carrot, two small lumps of coal, and a few pebbles.

Random Guy

I met a random guy. There was a tear in one of his eyes—another glistened on the back of his hand. He told me his story. It was a sad one. His dad beat the hell out of him until he was grown and big enough to defend himself.

He didn't know who he was; he made some bad decisions. He married a woman who he thought could answer his questions. She made vows and then, over time, broke them—every one.

He worked and reared children. Sometimes he hears from them. It took decades to realize that she had no answers.

Now he's alone; he's old and alone. I didn't like his story, but it's his; I won't judge. Then he told me that he...is me. Damn.

The Search

There's a story for which I'm searching. It has a name, and a draw. It will reach down into your gut and grip it with talons. It strains the sea from your eyes, and fills your mind with visuals—a montage reminiscent of times and experiences past, and those never lived, but could have been if one had the balls.

Taking you by the scruff of the neck, it drags you into places where dreams are found and forgotten, where flames touch your loins, and you run like the wind. Reality goes sideways, and the only way back is to stop, to stop reading, but you can't—you can't go back, not just yet.

Shorts: A Moratorium On The Ordinary

You may contact the author at:
stevenreeddahlquist@gmail.com